SPROCKET & THE GREAT NORTHERN FOREST

The Sprocket Sagas

—— BOOK 1 ——

With Added Dragon Facts

BRYAN PENTELOW

authorHOUSE®

AuthorHouse™ UK
1663 Liberty Drive
Bloomington, IN 47403 USA
www.authorhouse.co.uk
Phone: 0800.197.4150

Published by AuthorHouse 04/15/2015

ISBN: 978-1-5049-4001-6 (sc)
ISBN: 978-1-5049-4000-9 (hc)
ISBN: 978-1-5049-4002-3 (e)

Print information available on the last page.

<u>Dedicated to</u>

Sophie, Francesca, Thomas, Gabrielle and Harry
I hope you read this and like it.

CONTENTS

CHAPTER 1

A Delivery and a Discovery

It was a black and oily night, the sort you get in the back end of November, when clouds slime down off the fells trying to make up their minds whether to rain, sleet or simply hang around aimlessly as fog.

Blaggard the crow sat on a telephone pole by the tow path of the Great Eastern Canal, and humped his feathers against a nasty little breeze which sidled round the corner of Number 4 plant with chemicals on its breath. Blaggard coughed, and a hunched figure in a glistening black rain cape with the hood up froze in its furtive progress along the tow path, and pressed closer into the shadows of the corrugated iron fence. The figure bent deeper into the gloom and clutched a shoebox tied with hairy string tighter under its arm. The shoebox clicked and ticked quietly. The crow watched the rain cape as it greased past his telephone pole and edged round a bulge in the fence where the nails had rusted through, and a pile of old car tyres inside had fallen over and pushed the rusting sheets out.

Just as the figure slid from sight round the curve of the fence a soul rending screech split the night, and a bolt of black lightening ripped along the towpath. The rain cape jumped two feet into the air, staggered backwards, teetered along the worn edge stones of the canal, caught its balance and finally slumped against the fence where it lay wheezing horribly.

"Evil cat!" thought Blaggard "Always where it shouldn't be. Serves it right!"

With his right eye the crow watched the ragged shadow of Gertcha the Eurochem factory cat, slow, stop, spit and then slink into the gloom of the railway bridge with a last flash of malevolent yellow eyes.

Meanwhile with his left eye he watched the dark figure as it scrabbled at a loose piece in the fence and rammed the shoebox into the resultant gap. This done, it pushed the sheet back and scuttled out of sight round the corner into Pudding Founders Lane.

"Interesting!" thought Blaggard "Very Occult." (Crows think like this, believing themselves to be magical and closely associated with the Dark Arts, but really they're just large, black birds with over active imaginations). The crow carefully scratched an itch with one long claw, ruffled his feathers, then taking an extra firm grip on the pole with both feet, dozed off.

Dawn didn't break that morning, it sort of cracked in several places then dissolved into the cold grey drizzle which efficiently soaked everything then lurked about on the edges of things waiting for a passing neck to drip down.

Mr Brassroyd pulled on a fresh pair of dark blue overalls with artfully placed black stains, which even the best efforts of Gomersall's Industrial Laundry Service (pickups Mondays, deliver back Fridays same week) couldn't shift. Bending over with much muttering and puffing he pulled on and laced up his large boots with steel toecaps and best quality hobnails in soles and heels, then struggled into an industrial strength tweed jacket. He tied a thick grey wool muffler round his neck, tucked it into the front of his collarless striped shirt, pulled an oily flat cap firmly onto his head and stumped down the back stairs of number 7 Pudding Founders Lane to face the trials of a new day. He squeezed past several stacks of magazines and his large black bicycle to pick up the post from the mat inside the front door. Picking his way back along the hall towards the kitchen he sorted through the pile. Free offer, 'nother offer, more bumph, two brown envelopes from the Ministry of nosey devils wanting more facts and figures on how the small businessman kept the wolf from the door, free sample, letter from Grasping, Myther and Pry, appointed legal representatives for Eurochem International Plc. On entering the kitchen Mr. Brassroyd filed the post with yesterday's and the day before's behind the huge, gloomy, black marble clock on the top shelf of the dresser.

Once a week on Sunday afternoon he sorted, disposed of and occasionally replied to the pile which accumulated during the week, while he listened to the commentary on the Rugby League matches on the large walnut veneered radio in the front parlour.

Number 7 was the only cottage in Pudding Founders Lane and as far as anyone could remember always had been. What had happened to numbers 1 - 6 and any higher denominations had faded into the mists of time along with whom or what pudding founders were, and come to that how you founded a pudding. For Mr Brassroyd number 7 was home, office, workshop and repository for all the treasurers which he had salvaged over the years from the various piles of assorted scrap in the adjoining yard of Brassroyd Environmental (salvage and recycling) est. 1839. In living memory there had always been a Brassroyd at number 7 and Arthur Kitchener Mountbatten was the last of a long line. He sighed, unscrewed a large brass cap from a black iron tank by the black iron range, inserted a rectangular tin plate funnel with a mesh strainer in the bottom and carefully poured in two gallons of old sump oil. Removing the funnel he wiped it clean with a scrap of newspaper, screwed back the cap and proceeded to pump up the pressure with the long iron lever on top. One hundred and forty two strokes and a half for luck till the gauge reached the required setting. He opened the small, polished brass door at the base of the range, poured one fifth of a pint of paraffin onto three pages of last Saturday's Sports Advertiser and screwing then into a ball thrust them inside. Lighting a long match he applied the flame to the paper which flared quickly. Closing the door slowly, and turning the enamel tap marked Main Feed, he retreated to the other end of the kitchen, while the range emitted a succession of hisses which sounded like someone was prodding a bag of snakes with a stick, some pops and gurgles followed by a long choking gasp. The ensuing silence was terminated by a muffled thunder clap which caused several spiders to fall stunned from the rafters and signified ignition. Small pieces of rust rattled down the inside of the flue and a cough of oily smoke flipped off one of the small hot plates, as with a burbling roar the burner settled down to heating two and a quarter tons of cast iron, fancy brass, and enamel trim of the converted Pickersgill and Hains patented Home and Commercial Range. Mr Brassroyd rubbed his hands together and prepared to cook breakfast. In a corner of the yard under a pile of rusty car parts something clicked and ticked quietly.

The large black frying pan rang like a bell as Brassroyd dropped it onto the large hotplate alongside the brown enamel kettle, and from under the table came a rumbling cough as a large bow legged bull terrier cleared its tubes to face the day. It rolled from its basket, yawned like a hippopotamus and stretched itself from the blunt pink and black nose to the tip of its whippy, waggy tail. Mrs Mumbly was awake, and woe betides any foe that crossed her path. She blinked her small pink eyes, ran a yard of pink tongue round an impressive set of yellowish white fangs to make sure they were in the right place and all in order, and then waddled over to stand expectantly by the range in case Mr Brassroyd should drop any of his breakfast preparations. Mrs Mumbly liked breakfast. She liked crispy bacon. She adored black pudding. Corners of toast with Marmite on made her lick her long pink and black lips. But most of all she liked crisp, crunchy fried bread with lots of bacon fat, and the thought made her drool and wrinkle her nose, the better to sniff in the tempting sizzling aromas. Mr Brassroyd looked down as the dog banged its rock like head against his leg in the hope of an early starter.

"No breakfast for thee yet till thar's done thar mornin bits."

His back creaked as he bent and took firm hold of the thick leather collar with its brass studs and pulled the protesting dog to the back door which he opened and helped her over the door step with gentle pressure of his left boot. The door banged shut and Mrs Mumbly stood blinking and sniffing at the drizzle. She coughed and an echo returned from the crow on the telephone pole.

"Mornin Blaggard" thought Mrs Mumbly as she bowled bandy legged across the yard.

"Mornin Mrs Mumbly" thought the crow as it carefully rearranged its feet to face into the yard instead of across the canal.

"E's full of it today." thought Blaggard as through the kitchen door came the strains of the Amalgamated Bobbin Turners and Thread Pullers Trades Union Brass Band playing their stirring march 'Bobbins to the Fore' (conductor Ernest Grimsley, lead cornet Josiah Ramsbottom, pressed 1949).

"Aaahh!" Sighed Mrs Mumbly, relieving herself in an oily puddle by a bin marked Spark Plugs Asstd. in yellow wax crayon.

In a corner by Car Parts Various a flicker of movement caught her eye. With a low burbling growl Mrs Mumbly launched herself across the yard with all the grace of a main battle tank at full speed. Head down, teeth bared, she hurtled into a pile of crank shafts flinging them aside like match sticks, and sank her teeth into the tip of a flicking tail.

Something that looked like a bag made of moth-eaten carpet edged with razor-sharp claws shot vertically into the air and with a strangled yowl cleared the fence in one bound.

"Thut!" said Mrs Mumbly, daintily spitting a clump of rancid cat hairs from between her front teeth.

"That'll teach the foetid feline." grinned Blaggard watching a black and ginger streak scrabble over the chain link fence of Eurochem Number 3 Plant.

"Mmm," thought Mrs Mumbly "wonder what the mangy moggy was after this time?" as she waddled back across the yard and scratched at the door to be let in.

"Have to keep an eye on the murderous maggot."

In a shoe box behind Car Parts Various something ticked and clicked quietly.

The dog sat on her tail, her back legs sticking straight out as she leaned back against the warm range.

"Burp!" she said contentedly. Bacon rinds, three rounds of crisp fried Black Pudding, a dozen of her favourite biscuits, as hard as bullets and a thick slice of fried bread, crisp and golden brown, just as she liked it, filled her round pink and black mottled belly. "Burp!" she said again and her tail slapped happily against the stone flagged floor.

"S'no good makin yer sen comfy we got work t' do." Said Mr Brassroyd opening the door and squinting up at the drizzle

"Be dry by dinner". He pulled his cap more firmly onto his shiny bald head so that the fringe of white hair round his ears looked more like a frill on the cap than part of him. Mrs Mumbly waddled over to him and leaned against his leg her tail wagging slowly.

"Don't you lean agin me you got four legs o' yer own to stand on." he muttered stooping to scratch between the dog's ears. The bull terrier grumbled happily, deep in her chest then blundered into the yard to see what the day had to offer. They worked in silent companionship, sorting cans into two skips marked 'Tins Ferrous' and 'Tins Non Ferrous'. Mrs Mumbly was good at this, she could taste the sharp tang of tin plate on the steel ones and the aluminium ones made her teeth itch, so she sorted them into two piles and Mr Brassroyd scooped them up and put them into the skips. Occasionally she would lower her head and push a rusting cylinder block out of the way to get at another pile of cans. Like a four legged bulldozer, the muscles of her back and legs bunching and rippling, snorting through her wide flat nostrils and her chest rumbling like an old diesel engine, she would lean into the obstacle and it would just slide aside.

Blaggard watched from his pole, as motionless as a jet carving from Whitby, except for the slow blink of an eye. The rain was thinning and the wind had dropped to a breeze, which chased scraps of newspaper and dead weeds across the cobbles. Mrs Mumbly, on the other side of the yard, sniffed out some more cans tucked between an old tractor tyre and 'Car Parts Various'. She had just shouldered the tyre aside and was testing the first half dozen with her tongue when something made her pause. Tipping her head to one side and raising an ear, she listened carefully. Her nostrils flared, searching for the unusual within the everyday rust, battery acid, cat pee and mud. There it was again. Mrs Mumbly tipped her head the other way, her tail straight up and vibrating like a tuning fork. A soft gurgling growl mumbled in her chest as she walked her back legs to the left to change her direction and better triangulate a fix on the something.

Tick----click, click---------tick, ticker, tick, tick!

Mrs Mumbly took one step forward and nosed aside two crankshafts and an oil filter.

Ticker, ticker, click!

Her head cut through a drift of pistons like an ice breaker through pack ice.

Clickerty, clickerty, tick!

Ball and roller bearings tumbled in all directions as her spade-sized front paws probed deeper into the mound.

Click, ticky, ticky, tick!

Strong yellow white teeth fastened into a tangle of fan belts and the powerful legs reversed thrust.

Tug. Click! Haul. Tick! Pull. Clickerty tick! Muscles bunched, claws scrabbled for grip and with a mighty lunge the belts came free and unravelled like a swarm of maddened black serpents. It took Mrs Mumbly several seconds to untangle her legs, tail and ears, then she thrust her bullet head deep into the hole and blinked her pink eyes.

It was a shoe-box. She could smell traces of leather and she could see the hairy string which bound it. But the rest of the smell was confusing. What came from the inside of the box apart from a stream of worried clicks like Morse code with the jitters was a very strange scent indeed. It was like old piano keys and metal polish with tar and nappy powder. She hooked her teeth into the string and gently and firmly started to pull.

Blaggard swooped down onto 'White Goods Astd.' (Mr Brassroyd was very particular about his labelling) and perched on a rusty gas cooker.

"Very interesting." thought the crow as he watched the bull terrier pull first one way then the other, then press carefully on a corner of the knot in the string with its front paw to clear a protruding track rod end.

"Mumph!" said Mrs. Mumbly "A fat lot of help you are!" she thought "Sat up there passing dumb comments."

Her back legs found purchase on a piece of half buried angle iron and with a final tug the box came free.

"It's a shoe box." thought Blaggard, demonstrating his unerring ability to state the obvious.

"Mumph!" said the dog, her mouth full of bits of hairy string as she gnawed at the bindings.

"I hope you're not thinking of opening it? Could be full of dark and dangerous spells or occult objects with evil powers." thought the crow, standing on one leg to show how easy it was.

"And what would a cross between a coal scuttle and a feather duster like you know?" mused Mrs. Mumbly standing on four legs to show how stable it was. With a jerk of her head she snapped the last few strands of string and the box lay there, ticking and clicking. Very slowly the dog pushed the lid to one side, and revealed a box full of torn newspaper, wood shavings and sawdust which got right up her nose.

"Aaashoooo!" said Mrs. Mumbly with a sneeze like someone bursting a brown paper bag. When the ensuing cloud of packaging materials settled Blaggard and the dog stared at the egg which had been revealed. It was bigger than a goose egg and smaller than an ostrich egg, Mrs. Mumbly had seen both of those in a cabinet marked 'Eggs Asstd.' in the front parlour. Long and very pointed at one end, the egg was creamy white with wiggly red brown ridges all over it in a sort of hexagonal pattern. It ticked and clicked quietly to itself.

"Ha! Told you so" smirked Blaggard

"Oh, go feather your nest" thought the dog as with great care she picked up the egg in her mouth and waddled off towards the kitchen her tail wagging happily.

"And where d'yu' think you're goin'?" asked Mr. Brassroyd as he watched a wide wagging posterior disappear into the kitchen. "Might as well talk t' me self." He grumbled and went back to sorting a large tray of nuts, bolts and screws.

Mrs. Mumbly placed the egg gently on the cushion in her basket and nosed the blanket into a sort of nest round it. Then she pulled and pushed the basket into a warm corner between the range and the large, carved oak dresser containing all the bits of fine bone china which Mr. Brassroyd had found over the years. When she was satisfied that the egg was comfortable Mrs. Mumbly padded back into the yard pulling the door shut with the piece of rope Mr. Brassroyd had fixed to the latch for her.

She barrelled across the cobbles to where Mr. Brassroyd was still sorting his tray into a variety of biscuit tins.

"Better keep an eye on him" she sighed "Wouldn't know a self tapper from a pozidrive and his eyesight's not what it was."

She clambered onto an old ammunition box by the bench and watched him pick out a screw, then pushed the correct box towards him. Mr. Brassroyd obediently dropped the screw into it and picked up another. The dog nudged another tin and he placed it in that one. They worked on like this through the rest of the morning, the man picking screws, the dog nudging boxes. No words passed between them, none were needed, man and dog, the perfect team.

"Boring old buffers!" thought Blaggard and flapped back to his pole to spend a fascinating hour or so watching a dead rat float down towards Frampton's weir above Three Stage locks.

CHAPTER 2

Hatching and Research

In the kitchen the egg ticked and clicked and occasionally wobbled in its basket.

A small sunbeam squeezed between two pompous cloud banks and drifted down to settle on Mrs. Mumbly's nose. She sniffed then raised her head to blink her pink eyes at the sky. Then she banged her bony nose against the man's elbow and he stopped screw sorting and took a large silver watch from the top pocket of his overalls and flipped open the lid.

"Ah, pie and pint time. Look after t' yard for me old girl." He said slipping the watch back and pausing to scratch the hard flat space between the dog's ears. Mr. Brassroyd stumped of towards the gate and his lunchtime route to the Furnace Raddlers Arms (fine ales and stouts est. 1839) for a pint of 'Old Grubbers' dark mild and a plate of hot pork pie, mushy peas and a liberal splash of mint sauce. The dog hopped down from the box and waddled across the yard to 'White Goods

Asstd.', nosed open an old fridge and selected a large bone from her store. She always kept her bones in the fridge, it kept the rats away and she always knew where to find them.

"See thee Mountstaff."

"See thee Brassroyd. Pint o' t' usual?"

"Ay, an' a pie an peas if tha please." Mr. Brassroyd picked up his pint and carried it to the corner table by the fire and waited while Mountstaff, the landlord, shouted his order through the hatch to the ever present but never seen Mrs. Mountstaff in the kitchen. While he waited for the food to be passed through the hatch Mountstaff pulled himself a half pint of Thrapes best bitter then turned to pick up the steaming soup plate and carried both over to join his friend by the fire. He set down the plate and a spoon by the salt and pepper and lowered his ample posterior onto a stool.

"Tis proper slow these days. Not enough trade to feed a dray horse and that's a fact." He sighed as Brassroyd laid aside the Fells Clarion and attacked his pie and peas with a will. "How's your problems w'it t' conglomerate? Any more offers or threats?"

"'Ad a missive from them legal wallers again today, but it can wait till Sunday for the reading. I'm in no rush to scan their witterings," replied Brassroyd between mouthfuls.

"Tha should grab the money and pack it in. Tha's getting too old for mucking about in this cold and damp. Tha knows they'll get their way in t' end" muttered Mountstaff, reading the sheep prices at Pekinsfell sales which were as low as last weeks.

"'Ow would you feel if some big brewery tried to force you and the missus out of this place." said Brassroyd wiping his chin with a napkin. "Tha'd fight it tooth and nail. No there's allus been a Brassroyd at number 7 Pudding Founders Lane and there allus will be as long as I'm around. I'll not have them Stink makers taking my yard to fill with their leaky barrels and oily fluids. 'Tis bad enough having them next door. I 'av t' say you keep a good pint of mild and your Bethesda makes a grand pie and peas, if she weren't married I could offer her a good home."

"You think she'd come an live in that rats nest of yourn after the luxury she's been used to here? You've got a hope. "Get you another?" said Mountstaff, rising and lumbering back behind the bar.

"No, one's me limit of a lunch time you know that," smiled Brassroyd picking up the paper again as Mountstaff pulled himself another half.

"Well I'll never get rich off your wallet and that's a fact" grumbled the landlord, turning on his professional smile as the door swung open to admit another customer.

Meanwhile Mrs. Mumbly had settled down in the kitchen at number 7 for a good hours strenuous gnawing. She shuffled the bone around her mouth till it was settled at the right angle, then closed her jaws like a pneumatic car crusher. The pressure on the bone built up remorselessly till with a satisfying crack the knuckle end gave way and her teeth began to grind the splinters. A second crack broke the muttering quiet of the kitchen and she dropped the bone and stared at it accusingly. The bone lay there unconcerned and without so much as a twitch emitted another crack. Mrs. Mumbly snatched it up and administered a severe chewing then dropped it and scrutinised it closely. The bone lay there, not moving, and went crack twice more. Grabbing it by one end she blundered to the door, dropped the bone outside, slammed the door with her rump and retreated to the rug by the range to eye the entrance warily.

Crack! went the empty air and the dog shot bolt upright and peered cautiously round. Crack! She span round her teeth bared and tail ridgid. Nothing! Slowly she tensed her muscles, then hurled herself gape-jawed under the table.

Upside down with her paws paddling the air and her jaws clamped in a death grip on nothing, Mrs. Mumbly paused to take stock of the situation. With the slow dignity of an iceberg breaking free from the Arctic continent she rolled over and sorted her legs, tail and ears into their correct position.

Crack!

No rush this time, just a swivelling of ears. Crack!

Paws silently shuffled into position. A powerful killing machine poised to rip the intruder limb from limb.

Crack!

"Ha! Gotcha this time!"

Mrs. Mumbly sprang quivering with rage and stopped mid snap, her jaws aching from the pent-up forces driving to rip bone and sinew, and stared mesmerised at two large, black, limpid eyes ringed in cinnamon scented steam.

"What the?" thought Mrs. Mumbly.

"Yum, yum." thought the eyes.

Very slowly she relaxed her jaws and blinked at the eyes. They blinked back. She had never had pups but somewhere in her brain things fell into place and very gently she stretched forward and nosed a piece of shell from between two floppy, leathery ears. She began to lick it clean and the small creature seemed to like this and rubbed itself against her emitting a stream of clucks and chuckles while puffing tiny clouds of steam from its nostrils.

It was a most peculiar animal. The duck like head with long leathery ears sat on a short squat neck, which flowed into a body which looked like a badly inflated football. There was a long tapering tail and a sort of crest of floppy skin ran from the crown of its head to the tip of the tail. The hind legs were relatively large and powerful with three long pointed toes on each foot and something like a spur sticking out at the back. It sat on its hind legs and tail holding its smaller front legs, which had three pointed fingers and an opposed thumb each, clasped across its pink belly like a fat, contented old gaffer after a large Sunday lunch.

Mrs. Mumbly dragged over an old tea towel and placed all the bits of shell on it easing the small creature aside to pick out the pieces it had been sitting on. She was surprised how thick and tough they were.

"Poor little mite' she thought 'you must have had to work really hard to break out of there. I bet your starving after all that?"

"Yum, yum!'" thought the poor little mite.

A saucer from the cupboard under the sink was filled with milk from the jug in the fridge and pushed over to the basket. The poor little mite looked at the milk, then it looked at the dog, then back at the milk.

"Ah!" she thought "It doesn't understand how to drink from a saucer I'll get a spoon and feed it."

Standing on her hind legs she managed to pull a large, stainless steel dessert spoon from the draining board. Gripping it firmly in her front teeth she spooned up some milk and offered this to the mite which opened its beak very wide so she could push the spoon right in. Then it closed its beak and there was a plink sound, followed by a phut sound, followed by a gulp.

"Yum, yum!" thought the mite.

Mrs. Mumbly was very confused. In her mouth was the stub end of a spoon handle, on the floor was a small pool of milk and the mite was looking very pleased with itself. Of the rest of the spoon there was no sign. In her confusion she dropped the handle. The beak darted forward and a long, purple, forked tongue shot out, scooped up the metal, the beak snapped shut, there was a gulp and the mite looked even happier.

"Yum, yum!" it thought.

Mrs. Mumbly looked hard at the small creature which was bouncing up and down on its big back legs giving off 'Yum, yum.' thoughts like a radio-active isotope. She was not slow on the up take and waddled out into the yard, returning a few minutes later with a mouth full of assorted scrap metal, which she dropped in front of the mite. It fell upon the pile of bolts, rusty nails, springs and a short length of copper pipe with a mixed series of whistles, gulps and chuckles. Finally after licking up the last scrap of rust and a few stray iron filings, the tiny creature rocked back on its tail and burped contentedly. As its eyelids began to droop Mrs. Mumbly lifted it by the flap of loose skin at the back of its neck and placed it back in the blanket nest. Curling up with the tip of its tail wrapped round its nose the mite was instantly asleep, its small round belly rising and falling, and thin wisps of steam rising from its nostrils. The dog sat and watched it, her head on one side as she listened to the muted rumbles and gurgles from the mite's stomach. She had almost dozed off herself when a scrape of hob nails on cobbles heralded the return of the master from his lunch. As he entered the front door he was almost bowled over by a frantically enthusiastic bull terrier grumbling and tugging at the leg of his overalls.

"Calm down old lass. I know you're always pleased to see me but this is a bit much, I've been gone less'n an hour," said Mr. Brassroyd nearly falling over his bicycle as the dog tugged and butted him along the hallway towards the kitchen. Mrs Mumbly bounded back and forth from him to her basket trembling with excitement and impatience, till the man bent to examine the sleeping creature.

"Well, well! What have we got here?" he murmured, gently prodding the somnolent form with his finger. The form wiffled, gurgled, turned over and continued to sleep soundly. Mr. Brassroyd fumbled his spectacles onto his nose and peered closely at the tiny creature.

"My, my, would you believe it! I never expected to see one of these in all my life and a baby at that!" He straightened up and winced as his old back clicked in protest and, lifting his cap, scratched his bald head.

"Burp!" said the mite wriggling into a more comfortable position and continuing to snore softly.

"Come on old lass, better get the books down. This requires some serious looking up!"

He shuffled off into the front parlour and returned with arms full of thick, dusty, leather bound tomes, which he dumped on the kitchen table. After rummaging in several drawers he returned to the table with a notebook, a large magnifying glass and several pencils. He pulled out a chair, slumped into it and started to thumb through the pile of reference books. Starting with Hedges 'Legends of the Northern Fells', he progressed to Wortrights 'Serpents Compendium', the 'Observers Book of Mythical Creatures', via 'Wereworms and Warlocks' by W. Harpelbury-Pron and V.X. Barkwallie's 'By Scale and Sinew' (with full colour anatomical illustrations) to Pratt and Fortisque's 'I Dracus'. All this studying was interspersed with muttered comments such as "Not Dracus Vulgaris, wing buds are too high up." "Could be a lesser Swamp, but the colours all wrong." "Not a Welsh Red or an English Black. No tail horns so that rules out an Icelandic Berg Eater."

Mrs. Mumbly got bored as more books were fetched, opened and searched for clues, so she ambled out to the yard to find some choice morsels for when the mite woke up. She found an old carrier bag and wandered from pile to pile picking out some large metric nuts here and a tangle of small springs there, a ball of aluminium foil and some nice oily, blue black lathe turnings. On her return she found Mr. Brassroyd still furiously note making and page thumbing, while the mite had rolled onto its back, its rose tinted belly rising and falling in time with small whistling snores and thin plumes of steam. As she was tastefully arranging her collection on a large enamelled steel plate there was a hiccup from the basket and a pair of large black eyes peered over the rim.

"Yum, yum, yum!" thought the mite hopping out of the basket and proceeding to munch its way through the various mounds of sorted scrap. When it had licked the plate clean leaving not a trace of oil or rust, the mite sat back on its tail and eyed it from various angles by tilting its head this way and that. Finally, satisfied with its examination, it ate the plate as well. Then it sat back on its haunches burped twice and burbled contentedly.

"Well bless my soul!" gasped Mr. Brassroyd, who had watched the performance with open mouthed amazement. "You're a Dracus Metalicus Trogladytees, though whether you're a lesser or greater is impossible to tell till you grow a bit. Hmm, now, let's see. Dracus Metalicus. Ah yes, here it is. Scavenger dragon can grow to 4 feet (lesser) or 28 feet (greater) nose to tail. Males have crest from top of head to tail, females have crest only from shoulders to tail, so you're a little lad then. Cave dwelling, living mainly on seams of metal ore in rocks and dissolved mineral salts. Mainly nocturnal, poor flyers due to small size of wings, which develop in late adolescent phase. Known to produce flame, temperatures in excess of 1000 degrees C which it uses for cutting and refining food. Often found around battlefields in Arthurian times cutting up and consuming abandoned weapons and armour. Produces both droppings and regurgitated pellets, which are known to have many and various uses dependant on the animal's diet. Believed to have become extinct in the Middle Ages due to commercial hunting for use as a heat source in Iron Foundries and as raw material for alchemical research. Diet: Metals and metal ores though thought to be fairly omnivorous and have been known to lick resins and sap leakages from plants to supplement trace minerals and vitamins. Will drink any liquid containing mineral or chemical residues. Well you've certainly landed on your feet here young feller, there's no shortage of suitable food and drink for your sort and no mistake."

He watched the tiny dragon as it bounced from foot to foot as Mrs. Mumbly tried to lick it into shape.

"I think you'd better take it outside to do its business while I find a dust pan and brush to tidy up after it"

The dog gently picked up the dragon by the scruff of its neck and it dangled limply from her jaws clucking quietly as she ambled out of the door into the yard.

Blaggard had been studying a raft of garbage floating down the canal and as a consequence was unaware of the latest arrival at Brassroyd Environmental. His baleful gaze slid along the tow path to an out fall pipe from number 4 Plant where a viscous fluid was oozing into the water. 'Strange' he thought 'the colours are quite pretty if you ignored the occasional dead fish and the sulphurous smell. Not that there were many fish around these parts any more. There was a time when a crow could get good pickings from the worms, maggots and bread crusts left by fishermen, but since Eurochem had expanded there was nothing left worth fishing for. When the great stone edifice of Arkwright's Woollen Spinners had towered over the canal, its soaring arched windows more than one hundred feet tall to flood the teeming shop floors with day light, Batherby

Bridge had been a flourishing industrial and market town. The centre of the Five Fells district, it had been the trading hub for farmers, craftsmen and above all wool merchants. Thousands had surged through the huge wrought iron gates of the mill when the knocking-off hooter had shrilled, to fill the rows of stone roofed terraced houses, the shops, the pubs and the market with the gossip and trade of a living community. Steam trains had queued at the station platforms to take works outings to the seaside or the lakes, and left over sandwiches kept crows fat for weeks. At least that was the way old Grampus had told it, as hatchlings they had clung to the bare wind blasted branches of the home roost of the elms in The Remembrance Gardens. The young crows had been spellbound by his stories, for Grampus was a widely travelled bird. He had, in his youth, been swept north by winter gales from his soft southern birth nest, in London, where he had seen the sunset reflected in the magical Crystal Palace, and the evil shadows of enemy aircraft against the moon when the city had writhed in flames night after night. They had been great days for crows, rich pickings and people too busy to interfere. But Grampus was gone now, down the winds of time along with steam trains and the great mills. The rail tracks were rusty and weed choked, the station platforms and buildings empty and gutted after the failure of such ventures as Faggots R Us and Tripe Traditions Tasty Takeout. Terraces stood empty, broken windows gaped like decayed teeth in the litter strewn streets. Where thousands had thronged the mill floors, a couple of hundred lonely wraiths wandered the reeking, hissing galleries of Eurochem's five automated plants, checking a gauge here and turning a valve there. The all pervading gloom only broken by the thunder of the huge multi wheeled tankers which laboured back and forth to the distant motorway like mindless black beetles. A sad place, for sad people. The end of a road, which had been going nowhere for years. Blaggard clicked his beak and mournfully watched the garbage raft disappear under the arch of the railway bridge.

Mrs. Mumbly placed the dragon on the cobbles and stepped back to give it a chance to get its bearings. It sat there for a few minutes blinking its large black eyes, and then it looked round. Right round, a full 360 degrees. When its head had reached the starting point it seemed to lock in place and the rest of the little creature shuffled round to catch up. Satisfied that all seemed to be satisfactory it raised itself slightly. The tail stood straight up and began to tremble, its eyes crossed and it flexed its front paws. There was a faint tinkling sound then it scampered off towards a stack of old tyres. What was left behind was a neat cone of small cinders, which glowed briefly red then faded to ash grey. Mr. Brassroyd scuttled over with the dustpan and brush and swept up the cinders muttering "Yes, yes, just as I expected, seems fine, must have this looked at." He retreated to the kitchen where he emptied the contents of the pan into a brown envelope, sealed it down and placed it on the top shelf of the dresser.

Meanwhile in the yard the baby dragon skittered from stack to pile to heap, nibbling a rusty wire here and siphoning an oily puddle there. Mrs Mumbly sat on her tail, her back legs sticking straight out, head on one side, one ear up and one ear down watching the mite with loving pink eyes as it bobbed and scampered about its large flat feet plapping on the cobbles. She yawned cavernously, the weak winter sun drowsing her afternoon mood and scratched an itch on her belly. The dragon galloped round a bag of old socks and burrowed into a crevice between two piles of decomposing cardboard boxes. Now she saw him. Now she didn't! She sprang up with a jolt and thundered across the yard toward the boxes.

Seething with worry, Mrs. Mumbly began to claw at the boxes. "Oh dear! Where is it? It could be trapped! It could be squashed! Poor mite could be mortally injured! Oh bother!"

Blaggard glided down onto a tea chest and peered down a crack behind the heaps.

"If you mean this small fat lizard with the floppy ears? It's down here lapping up a pool of green slime which is leaking from a crack in the factory wall," thought the crow its head on one side to keep a beady eye on the mite, who was emitting an aura of 'yum, yum' thoughts.

Mrs. Mumbly tore into the boxes like a shredder on turbo boost, grabbed the dragon by the scruff of the neck and jerked it back into daylight and safety. She dumped it unceremoniously onto the cobbles and gave it a black and scolding look. The mite blinked up at her with a happy grin on its beak as its round belly gave off an alarming succession of pops, gurgles and hisses. The dog ran around frantically trying to spot anything medicinal, which might counteract toxic sludge ingestion.

A large bluebottle, wakened by the pale sunshine from its sleep in a rotting cauliflower, buzzed slowly across the yard. The small dragon's head snapped up, its beak tracking slightly off the fly and it sneezed. Twin jets of blue white flame shot out and neatly bracketed the bluebottle, which instantly became ash and drifted to the cobbles.

"Good Lord!" thought Mrs. Mumbly skidding to a halt.

"Good shot!" thought Blaggard "I reckon yon small worm packs enough artillery, to look after you and me, as well as it."

The mite beamed with pleasure and bounced up and down radiating 'again-again-again'. The crow picked up a piece of plastic egg carton with its claws and flicked it towards the dragon that promptly incinerated it in mid air. "Neat!" Next he picked up a worn bicycle brake block and tossed it in a high arc towards the bobbing, chuckling creature. The dragon tracked it, made a sort of chuff sound and two balls of incandescent fire flashed the block to a smudge of oily smoke, faster than you could blink.

"Very impressive!" Blaggard plucked up two large plastic washers and with a flick of his beak sent them soaring like a Frisbee towards the top of the telephone pole.

Chuff! Chuff! Went the dragon and two clouds of greasy black smuts drifted down to the cobbles. 'Gain-again-again' pulsed the tiny mite bouncing and skipping in circles.

"Enough!" thought Mrs. Mumbly, "too much excitement's not good for small things." She placed a large paw on the base of its tail to hold it still and taking a firm grip on its scruff lifted it into the air. Immediately the little dragon went as limp as a bag of jelly and the dog carried it back into the kitchen. Gently placing it in the basket she nudged the blankets round it then climbed in, curled round the mite and began to lick it between its leathery ears. In seconds the dragon was fast asleep, clucking and ticking to itself, its round pink belly still giving rise to the occasional menacing rumble.

Mr. Brassroyd had fetched more books and magazines and was deep in his research, only a muffled "well, well!" and "would you believe it?" to show he hadn't dozed off. Mrs. Mumbly put her head on her paws and closed one pink eye. The tiny Dragon snuggled up so close that one of the dog's pink and black lips drooped over the top of its head and a leathery ear was pressed against her teeth. In this fashion they snoozed into the evening.

Outside, on his telephone pole, Blaggard watched a dead pigeon float past and got down to some serious thinking.

Crows have a long memory, much longer than an individual crow; it's a sort of species memory. They can remember back through generations of crows, and there have been crows around tidying up the planet since before men came down from the trees. Blaggard locked his claws onto the pole and lapsed into a trance. His mind flowed down the streams of time searching for a fat lizard shape with floppy ears. It flowed past rubbish tips and bombsites, past plague pits and middens, across the battlefields of history till it hit a scene sliding from dusk to night. Here crows picked at dead horses and strutted across fallen banners and broken spears. Wounded moaned and pleaded for help and pity, their cries often cut short by a swift knife in the hand of a human scavenger grubbing for coin or chalice amongst the detritus of pride and strife. Desolation and misery followed in the wake of war, where once honour and courage had been the battle cry of both sides. Looking through the eyes of his ancestors Blaggard surveyed the carnage, searching for a telltale flame or scuttling shape. There! There it was over by a stand of leafless trees, a bright glow, gone almost as soon as it bloomed. The crow leaped into the air and glided silently to one of the barren branches where it alighted and scanned the litter of war. Nothing moved except the flap of a torn surcoat in the night wind, then a brief flash of blue fire and the visor of a discarded helm fell with a muted clang. What Blaggard had at first thought was a pile of rags by a corpse moved, changing its shape against the pale glow of the last remnants of the day. Outlined clearly for a few seconds were the leathery ears and the duck shaped head as it darted forward to snap up the visor. The flame flashed again and the rest of the helm was gulped down. Ragged wings partly unfurled for balance as the creature scuttled to a breastplate which it flashed into segments and quickly swallowed. The crow sat silently on the branch for some time and watched the dragon cut up and devour swords, axes, halberds and shields. It never went near any of the bodies but took only the metal devoid of human flesh. Finally Blaggard withdrew from his ancestor and returned to his pole. 'So that's what it was, after all this time, one of the old legends had walked out of the past and into his back yard. Well, well how fascinating' mused the crow. He would have to keep a very close eye on this, after all legends were a crow's business and should not be left to bumbling old gaffers and daft dogs.

Mrs Mumbly stirred, stretched, yawned like a barn door and plodded over to the table where soft snores from the figure slumped over the pile of books and magazines indicated that research had come to a temporary halt. A stream of clicks and chuckles from the basket heralded the awakening of the dragon and a pair of dark eyes blinking over the rim confirmed this. The dog returned to her charge, picked it up and made for the door and into the yard. Dumping the dragon on the cobbles she pressed a front paw on its tail to prevent it from rushing into the night in search of food and looked sternly into its limpid eyes.

"Now don't you go getting lost, and come when I bark, no more frightening the living daylights out of me." The mite gurgled and nodded its beak. Satisfied that the message had got through she lifted her paw and the tiny creature scampered off into the gloom. A shadow swooped down and landed on the iron boot scraper next to her.

"Do you realise what you've got there?" smugness shone from the crow's eyes as it leaned forward.

"Yes, it's a poor little lost soul with no Mum to look after it and keep it safe." mused the dog its pink eyes all misty as it followed the shadowy form bouncing and hopping around the yard.

"No you daft canine, it's a scrap dragon, a legend, an extinct species, not been seen in these parts or any other for hundreds of years!"

"I know that. Brassroyd looked it up in his books, but it's still a babe and needs its Mum and that's me! I shall look after it and keep it safe and give it a warm nest in my basket."

While this heated exchange was in progress a ragged shape oozed under the fence and crept on silent paws from shadow to shadow. Gertcha was on his never ending mission to revenge himself on the hated man and dog. Like all cats he followed the golden rule of never messing on your own doorstep and consequently took great pleasure in relieving himself in the scrap yard and causing chaos by overturning boxes and toppling piles of scrap whenever possible. But tonight he had spotted a new possibility for mayhem. He stalked the small bobbing creature, getting closer with every furtive move. Another couple of slithering runs and he would be near enough to spring. Then the fur would fly and another interloper onto his territory would be vanquished and he could settle down on top of a nice high stack to watch the dog run round like a headless chicken barking fit to burst. The tiny dragon paused and sniffed the air. It stretched up on its back legs and looked all round. As its gaze passed over the cat filled gloom, Gertcha froze, but the eyes passed on without a pause, and then after executing a peculiar circular shuffle continued on its bouncy exploration. The cat made a fast dash to a pile of plastic buckets climbed silently to the top and coiled itself to spring. He launched himself in a high arc, claws out, ears back, fangs bared and dropped soundlessly onto the bobbing shape. So easy! Except the shape side stepped, snapper up its beak and suddenly Gertcha was in the middle of a boiling ball of flame. In mid air he flipped to land a yard away on severely singed paws. With a yowl of startled terror and rage he took off over the fence trailing a plume of smoke, which smelled as if someone had been burning some really disgusting old rugs. The dragon encouraged his exit with a pair of fireballs aimed to miss but close enough for the heat to be felt. Dog and crow rushed across the yard alarmed by the sudden conflagration. What they found apart from a nasty singed smell, was the mite rocking back and forth on its tail while it scanned the top of the fence and rootled soot from its nostrils with the forked tip of its tongue. In the weeds at the back of Plant 4 a very angry and puzzled tom cat tried to sharpen its fire blunted claws on a fence post and scratched and licked at its singed and blackened fur. Its mind boiled with spite and malice as it slunk away to work out a means of getting even, if not actually one up.

Despite the fussing from both crow and dog, they could find no sign of injury to the dragon, which was grinning all over its beak and bouncing up and down.

"Did you see it? Did you see what it did? One ball of flame caught that stinking cat in mid leap! Just enough to singe its coat and whiskers. Then two more to make sure it ran. Brilliant!" The crow hopped from foot to foot with excitement. "It could have cut that cat in half, but all it did was singe it. What control! What accuracy! And all in a split second!"

But what Blaggard didn't realise, and the dragon knew full well, was that he had seen Gertcha lurking in the shadows, and had tracked the cat's approach with those silly floppy ears, hearing the scratch of the claws at the moment of leap, which had enabled it to calculate the angle of drop and snap off the fireball at just the right moment. The predator had not stood a chance from the moment his filthy, burr encrusted coat had grated against the corrugated iron sheet as he had slid under the fence. Scrap Dragons may have been considered extinct but they were certainly no-one's free lunch, and more than a match for any alley cat. Having sniffed and licked the small creature all over and found no sign of damage Mrs Mumbly sat back and looked long and hard at it. The dragon grinned back then bobbed off to find more tasty morsels.

Dog and crow sat in companionable silence watching the shadowy shape flit about the yard, occasionally thrown into sharp silhouette as it flamed a large piece of scrap into more manageable chunks. Stars came out and a thin, sharp moon played hide and seek amongst the wind shredded clouds. Eventually the dog gave a short bark and the mite scampered to her and meekly lowered its head so she could pick it up and carry it off to bed.

"See you in the morning then," thought the crow as it flapped off to its post, and as the kitchen door swung shut the yard was left to the scuttling of rats and the silent spinning of spiders.

The night slid past with the clouds across an icy moon, and deep in the shadows Gertcha wrought his evil by clawing long scratches on anything he could and peeing on every convenient corner, and finally leaving a small, steaming, evil smelling pile on the back door mat. Blaggard watched in disgust as the mangy animal slimed under the fence back into the weed-choked perimeter of the Eurochem site.

'Pathetic, twisted creature,' thought the crow 'One day he will push his luck too far and run out of lives!'

Blaggard dozed, and his dreams were filled with long forgotten battlefields haunted by the pale blue flash of flame and the scurrying of scaly feet.

Morning crawled over the edge of the moor and slouched along the canal bank, making the sparrows cough by breathing damp mist up their beaks. A mongrel padded along the towpath, paused to relieve itself against Blaggard's telephone pole, and after catching up on the news by sniffing all round the base, wandered off around the curve of the fence towards the railway bridge. The crow shifted his balance onto one leg and proceeded to sort out his feathers with his free set of claws. While he was deeply involved in ferreting out an itch under his left wing, a searing and obscene thought burned through the morning. Mrs Mumbly had come out to sniff the morning and found what Gertcha had left on the mat the previous night. As Blaggard straightened up to bid good morning to her, a scaly duck shaped beak appeared between the dog's front legs and a jet of purple fire enveloped the stinking pile. It was literally all over in a flash. Where the pile had been was a small cone of white, odourless ash and the mat was not even singed. Dog and crow stared in amazement as the small dragon squeezed into sight, hopped over the ash and scampered round the yard lapping some oil here and gobbling some rust there.

Meanwhile back in the kitchen Mr Brassroyd was preparing breakfast and mulling over the details he had gleaned from his researches the previous day. According to D. W. Cleg's

Flora and Fauna of Dragon Lands, the droppings of scrap dragons were wonderful for mixing with compost to grow prize winning pot plants and vegetables. Depending what the animals had been eating their droppings contained all sorts of nutrients and trace elements, and because they were baked so hard in the heat of the dragons lower intestine the fertiliser was concentrated and slow release. The book had recommended just two pellets to a kilo of well rotted compost to produce roses the size of cabbages and onions like footballs, and the author maintained that their taste was better than any other vegetables. Brassroyd could picture the scrap yard blooming like the Garden of Eden with three foot long marrows and pea pods as long as your fore arm, but first he had to deal with the problem of its current contents. He hummed quietly to himself as he sliced up a particularly fine black pudding and slid the pieces into the cheerfully sizzling frying pan. In the yard a breath of frying bacon sidled up Mrs Mumbly's nostrils and she gave a short bark which brought the baby dragon galloping towards her, a length of old mains cable rapidly disappearing into its beak. She took hold of the mite by the scruff of its neck and in seconds had run into the kitchen. Having dumped her charge in the basket, she assumed her normal breakfast time position, close to Brassroyd and the range, and stared fixedly at the handle of the frying pan. On his post Blaggard resumed his inspection of the canal.

'Typical!' he thought 'dogs are nothing but an appetite on legs. Give 'em a sniff of food and their minds go blank of everything but thoughts of feeding their faces.' At that moment a particularly rancid raft of decomposing rubbish floated into view round the corner of Number 4 Plant and the crow swooped low over the oily water, snatched a foetid titbit from the pile, and soared back to enjoy this bounty of nature which the canal had brought him.

CHAPTER 3

Nasty Plans by Bad People

In an office in a city, well away from the Eurochem factory, several grey men in grey suits and hard expressions stared at several pages of figures which told a grim tale of toxic waste build up and falling profits. Reginald Snidely, chairman of Eurochem International, turned his shiny bald head towards his finance director and fixed him with a withering stare.

"Well! Why are the costs up and the profits down?"

The finance director, a shrunken man who knew the cost of everything and the value of nothing, shuffled his papers and blinked at the chairman through his rimless glasses.

"The cost of disposal is rising rapidly due to the amount of toxins produced by the new process for making short life plastics and the distance we have to transport it in order to have it safely re-processed Sir Reginald," he wheezed.

"What do you mean re-processed! Dump the stuff somewhere local. That area is peppered with old quarries and mine shafts, there's supposed to be one under that property next door to Number 4 Plant, haven't you evicted the old fool that owns it and taken it over yet?" Sir Reginald had a very short fuse and his neck was turning red, a bad sign for all concerned.

The finance director did some rapid calculations and a nasty smile formed on his thin bluish lips.

"I estimate that if we simply piped the effluent into the old mine workings we could not only reverse the downturn but increase the margin by a further two hundred percent."

The chairman's eyes swivelled like searchlights and fixed on a foppish young man with a large Adam's apple and a weak chin.

"What are you and your crew of wasters doing about acquiring that junk yard?"

"Well Sir Weginald, we have made appwoaches to the local council for a compulsowy purchase order to be placed on the pwoperty and our legal chaps have sent a letter with a most genewous offer for the purchase of the site."

"Purchase? Purchase?" the chairman's ears had now gone red and eruption was imminent.

"I don't want to buy the place I want to own it! Put the frighteners on the old fool and clear him out. Good Lord, do I have to do everyone's thinking for them? I want that yard in our hands by the end of the month or some of you will be looking for new jobs. Now get out and make it happen. No excuses will be tolerated! Do you hear me?" The chairman had risen from his chair and was all but blowing steam from his ears. His face was bright red and a vein in his temple could be seen pulsing. The assembled grey men beat a hasty retreat from the boardroom and scurried to their offices to rapidly plan the demise of Brassroyd Environmental.

Numbers were dialled and voices murmured about favours owed and monies paid out. How certain facts leaked to certain people could prove very embarrassing unless actions were taken and things happened. In the corridors of Northern Local Government figures hurried back and forth and hushed conversations were held in corners and very private rooms. Topics such as election expenses and certain trips abroad to the warmer and more expensive parts of the world, which had not dented the beneficiary's bank accounts, were mentioned. Panic sloshed about like acid and pressure was applied in certain quarters. Desired courses of action were made crystal clear. Rules were bent, and by-laws were twisted till eventually a very official series of documents emerged from a number of municipal departments and were consigned to the postal service for delivery to number 7 Pudding Founders lane.

CHAPTER 4

A Visit to the Chemist

Blissfully unaware of all the heavy corporate activity being brought into focus on it, the business of Brassroyd Environmental commenced another days trading. It was however somewhat different as the new member of the team was making his presence felt.

Brassroyd leaned on the handle of a large stokers shovel and watched the small scrap dragon scamper about the yard. Here it paused to gobble up a scatter of rusty nails, then it pattered a few yards and munched its way through a tangle of old steam piping. Back and forth it skipped, pausing occasionally to slurp up a puddle of oily fluid or slice up a choice morsel with a flash of blue-white flame, and everywhere it passed the yard seemed tidier and the cobbles seemed to shine with a gloss they had never had even when newly laid.

Mrs Mumbly sat in her favourite place on an old leather car seat under an overhang of corrugated iron, which served to shade it from the sun or more often shelter it from the rain, which seemed to fall at least five days out of every seven and eight months of the year. To be fair the climate was varied by fogs, smogs, drizzle, frosts, snow and winds which cut through even the thickest overcoats as if they were string vests.

You wouldn't think summut so small could put away so much scrap and not burst." said Brassroyd to no one in particular.

"Ah well he's a lot of growing to do and it takes a lot out of a mite does growing." mused the dog, her eyes following the duck and swoop of the small scaly head as a scatter of washers and a small coil of barbed wire were snapped up. After a further ten minutes of eating the little dragon sat down and seemed to drop into a doze, while from his insides came the most alarming gurgling and popping. Occasionally he would shudder and wobble from side to side and puffs of green smoke would rise from the flame vents on the top of his beak. Finally he gave a loud sneeze and a series of coughs and several glowing pellets fell from his open mouth and lay steaming on the cobbles. He went through this process twice more then stood up, shook his ears vigorously and scampered off to sample more of the yards' fine fare. Brassroyd carefully shovelled up the pile of pellets which had now cooled and dropped them carefully into a large glass jar which he held up to the light and examined carefully.

"Well I'll be dammed!" he exclaimed. "Mind the shop old girl, I must take this to Pongo Feather at the chemists," and with that he disappeared into the kitchen clutching the jar. The sound of the front door closing confirmed that he had left on his errand.

Brassroyd made his way along the High Street, the glass jar clutched in a patchwork leather shopping bag, while back in the yard dog and crow watched the small dragon continue its cycle of eat, gurgle, cough up pellets and eat again.

Feathers Pharmacy and purveyors of surgical appliances since 1906 occupied a prime site on the corner of High Street and Salamanca Road. Pongo Feather, so named since school days due to an interest in chemistry, which focused on what mixed with what would make the worst and longest lasting smells, was a long standing friend of Brassroyd. They both had a passion for industrial history and strange old machines.

Entering the shop Brassroyd plonked himself on a chair in the corner between a rack of herbal cough lozenges and a display of surgical supports, the illustrations for the use of which seemed to be a cross between a guide to medieval torture and the sort of magazines which Gupter Patel kept on the top shelf of his newsagents. He waited patiently while the queue of nature's frail and suffering coughed, wheezed and whispered their tales of woe and list of symptoms to Cheryl, the buxom rosy cheeked lass who bellowed their requirements, however private and embarrassing to Pongo in the preparation room at the back where he counted pills, filled bottles and measured powders for the relief of the stricken. Having read the instructions to the relevant sufferer and rung the money into the till Cheryl bade them farewell with a cheery "Get well soon" as they shuffled scarlet-necked from shop. When the queue of the morning's walking wounded had departed, and Cheryl was busying herself rearranging a display of corn plasters, Brassroyd nipped round the counter and into the back room.

Pongo looked up from a potion he was mixing and smiled to see his old mate.

"See thee Brassroyd. What brings thee out this morning? Not bowel trouble I hope?"

"Don't be disgusting Feather. I'll thank thee that me bitts are working fine. Thar'll never get rich on me."

"That's true," said Feather shaking his head "I say a little prayer of thanks each day that folks round here at least have the decency to be properly ill once in a while. Now, what can I do you for?"

Brassroyd extracted the jar and a large brown envelope and placed it on the work bench.

"I need these analysing and I don't want the whole world to know about it so don't be letting Foghorn Freda out there be nosing around."

"Right you are then." muttered Feather and slid the jar and envelope into a deep draw under the bench. "It'll be an afterhours job then, I'll see thee in back bar of the Raddlers before closing time."

Brassroyd made to leave but Feather grabbed his arm and thrust an empty pill box into his hand.

"Take this it'll give nosey drawers sommat to think on." Feather ushered his pal out of the door "Take two with each meal and the swelling will soon go down," he said grinning knowingly at Cheryl who was craning her neck to see over Cuthbert's Chloridine Cough Cures.

Brassroyd hurried back to the yard in time to take delivery of four bins of ferrous, and two of nonferrous turnings from a spotty youth who drove the van for Grimsdyke Grinders, Fettlers and Turners on the station trading estate. He noted the weight of each drum as the youth swore and sweated as he heaved them on and off the black iron scales, then signed the docket and folded the note and tucked it in his overall pocket for entry into the ledger later.

"The old sod says he's got twenty gallons of oil slurry needs clearing. If you'll take it, he'll drop it off and you can knock it off the scrap account." The youth ducked to avoid the back handed swipe Brassroyd aimed at him and dodged into the van.

"That's Mr Grimsdyke to you. Show some respect for your betters you spotty oik!" shouted Brassroyd after the rapidly departing van as it skittered across the cobbles and roared off up Pudding Founders lane.

Having closed and locked the gates he unpegged the door and dog and dragon barrelled into the yard. The mite scampered straight to the new bins and bounced up and down excitedly.

"No!" said Brassroyd firmly "That's got resale value. You stick to the mixed junk over there. Keep an eye on him old girl and see he don't gobble what little profit there is in this business."

The team worked steadily for the rest of the afternoon and, as evening slid damply off the moor, they surveyed the results of their efforts.

Brassroyd had to admit things were improving. The stock of sorted metals which could be reprocessed had increased and the mountain of mixed junk, though still vast was getting smaller. The little dragon had a prodigious appetite and the amount of dragon by-products, both ash and pellets, was growing in the two stainless steel bins he had cleaned out specially.

Wiping his hands on some cotton waste Brassroyd went into the kitchen. He put a pan of water on for the spuds and putting a blob of lard into a roasting tin he hooked open the oven door and slid it in to warm. He washed his hands thoroughly using hard yellow soap and scouring powder. He then got a pack of six fat sausages from the old Westinghouse catering sized fridge, separated them, pulled out the roasting tin and popped them in to brown. Next he peeled the spuds and put them in the now boiling water. He mixed a pudding batter from eggs, flour and milk and left it to stand on the side. A smaller pan was filled with water and put on for the greens. Removing the roaster again he carefully spaced out the bangers and poured in the batter mix and replaced it in the oven. Thick brown gravy was mixed to his special recipe including two spoons of mustard, one of marmite and a splash of brown ale from the remains of last night's bottle. Then he chopped half a cabbage and placed it in the small pan.

Mrs Mumbly barged into the kitchen drawn by the smell of baking and the delicious scent of thick gravy. She licked her lips expectantly and rumbled in her throat, her tail wagging.

Brassroyd chuckled "Not long now lass. Get the nipper in and bed him down for the night."

Supper passed in companionable silence apart from the clatter and scrape of Mrs Mumbly gnawing her favourite burnt bits from the roasting tin.

Brassroyd pulled on his coat and looked in to check on the animals. The dragon was asleep in the dog basket its front paws over its eyes and tail curled round beak, horrid bubblings coming from its insides. Mrs Mumbly lay on her back by the range, her black spotted pink belly rising and falling to her slow breathing, all four paws in the air. He smiled at the picture of contentment and went off to meet Pongo in the Raddlers back bar.

For the Raddlers the front bar was heaving. Two old codgers sat glowering at each other over a death or glory dominoes game, grinding their toothless gums in concentration and making their pints last all night. A damp raincoat and cap in the corner raked myopically through the racing results muttering dark curses against bookmakers, bent jockeys and trainers on the take, damming them all to the eternal fires. The salesman at a table on his own, ignored pointedly by the locals, stared blankly at the Times crossword and wished he'd bought the Sun, trying to put off the awful moment when he would have to turn in to the cold damp bed in the pub's only room to let.

Brassroyd shunned the excitement of the cribbage game which had just erupted into sullen dispute over whether it should be fifteen six and one for his knob, or fifteen twelve as the claimant maintained. He sidled down the passage to the back bar and peered round the door to find it empty except for the landlord's flatulent spaniel which lay steaming by the fire giving off an odour of boiled dish cloths.

"Pint o dark?"

"Aye"

Mountstaff's instinct for a regular never failed. He could tell by the creek of their boots who had come in. He pulled a pint of Old Grubbers and brought it through.

"Not like you to be in ere" said Mountstaff "Sommat up?"

"Me and Pongo got business" muttered Brassroyd tapping the side of his nose with his finger.

"Oh, right, I'll keep t'others out. Let me know when you're done".

There was the sound of footsteps in the passage and Mountstaff went into the front bar and returned moments later with a gin and peppermint which he placed in front of the muffled figure who had slumped next to Brassroyd. Feather unwrapped himself and took a sip from his glass.

"I don't know how you can drink that stuff" muttered Brassroyd.

"It keeps out the cold and clears me tubes, anyway to business,"

Feather rummaged in one of the deep inside pockets of his overcoat, which seemed to have been built rather than tailored. To watch Feather out on a winters day, was like seeing a man going for a walk in a small shed which moved to keep up with him. His mother had always bought his cloths a size too big so he could grow into them, and Feather had stuck to this rule. The problem was, he had stopped growing many years ago, so now had to be careful not to turn round quickly or his clothes remained facing the other way. He finally extracted a sheet of paper which he slapped triumphantly on the bar.

"The report!" he said "and what a report. Do you know these are the most complex substances I have ever analysed?"

"But what's it do?" asked Brassroyd squinting through his glasses at the close typed sheets full of chemical formula.

"That's the problem." breathed Feather "almost anything! Chemically it's inert. It don't burn, it don't corrode things and it don't smell. But it's so full of unusual chemical combinations it ought to vibrate and glow in the dark, neither of which it does by the way. It does nothing as far as I can see.

"Great!" muttered Brassroyd "I've been carefully collecting dragon droppings and now you tell me they're no damn use."

"Not exactly." said Feather "The powder has a nonexistent coefficient of friction."

"How's that? Speak English won't you," growled Brassroyd.

"I mean that anything placed on a surface coated with this powder would slide right off. It's like a perfect air bearing. Machines with bearings coated with this would be almost 100% efficient! As for the pellets, your guess is as good as mine," explained Feather.

They spent another hour discussing Feather's findings and their implications, then the spaniel broke wind, and the pair made a hurried exit followed by a cloud of rancid air. Mountshaft watched them go as he rearranged the smears on a pint glass with a threadbare tea towel.

"I'll never retire on what that pair spend," he sighed and put the glass back on the shelf. "Haven't you lot got homes to go to?" he said to the remaining regulars, who took the hint and shuffled out.

Feather had crushed two of the three pellets he'd been given for analysis, the third, Brassroyd tossed into the yard, he could sweep it up tomorrow with any others. What he was going to do with them now he hadn't a clue. The pellet went Plink as it bounced off a cobble and landed in a large pot that contained a sorry looking geranium. He put the envelope containing the rest of the ash in a drawer with Feather's report, locked the door and went to bed.

A shaft of cold sunlight shone into the yard catching the clouds on the hop and illuminating a strange sight. Mrs Mumbly and the mite were the first to witness it and it made the dog bark in surprise, which in turn woke Blaggard and brought Brassroyd to the door.

"Oh my goodness!" thought the crow, and the man said it.

There in a scatter of broken pot shards and sprung cobbles stood a four foot geranium bush covered in deep crimson blooms. Its trunk, for trunk it was, nothing that thick could be called a stem, was 150mm in diameter, or in Brassroyd's terms six inches. The leaves were dark green with sort of purple edges and the only way to describe it was vigorous.

The small dragon danced around it piping excitedly and blowing pink smoke rings.

"Well I never!" exclaimed Brassroyd.

"In the middle of November," thought the dog.

"Made a mess of the pot," mused the crow.

"Yum, yum," thought the dragon and shovelled up some rusty nails which it swallowed and licked its beak with its forked tongue.

Brassroyd carefully examined the soil round the base of the geranium. Close to where the roots had sprung the ancient cobbles, and burrowed into the black earth beneath, was a husk which had been the pellet he had discarded the night before. Nothing was left but a tracery of what appeared to be fine metal wires which crumbled to dust as he touched them. He frowned and went back inside, dug out the remains of the other pellets and his large magnifying glass. Careful study of the fragments revealed a similar filmy mesh, proving in fact that the pellet had dissolved into the soil of the pot.

Returning to the yard he found the small dragon cross-eyed and coughing. It stretched its neck, coughed twice more, and spat two more pellets onto the cobbles. Brassroyd snatched them up and cursed as the hot objects burned his fingers. The dog looked at him, head on one side, then at the crow who squawked and flew off. The dragon scampered round the yard munching any scrap which took his fancy and occasionally coughing up pellets or leaving small cones of glowing ash in his wake. Mrs Mumbly pointed out each deposit and Brassroyd collected them into the two stainless steel cans.

Eventually the mite became tired and the dog carried him into the kitchen and laid him in the dog basket. He curled up in his usual circular fashion and went to sleep emitting the strange clickings and rumblings which indicated his digestive system was working fine. Dog and man stood watching the small sleeping creature. Brassroyd lifted his cap and scratched his shiny bald pate.

"You know old girl, when he's curled up like that he looks just like a little cog wheel. I think we'll call him Sprocket." The dog grumbled in agreement. It seemed right. So Sprocket it was. The dragon slept on not knowing or caring that his naming ceremony had taken place.

In a valley, several miles away over the moors, a number of crows swooped and scratched through a patch of mixed woodland, the only remnant of the great forests which had once marched across this wilderness. Here an acorn, there a beech mask, now a conker, there a hazel nut, each crow brought its find to a small clearing where Blaggard stood guard over the growing contents of a plastic carrier bag. By evening they had a fair collection and with a level of co-operation rare in corvines the bag was lifted and flown back to the yard. None of the towns' inhabitants noticed the flock of crows and their burden against the dark glowering overcast. Heads down against the wind driven drizzle they hurried home to the comforts of fireside or central heating. Blaggard pulled the bag under the geranium, now two meters tall, but with flowers closed for the night then returned to his perch on the telephone pole.

CHAPTER 5

Developments

Things had been moving elsewhere. Not satisfied with glacial progress of municipal sanctions, missives had been sent to the murkier sections of the business world, which operated on the edge of or beyond the law. Deniable instructions were issued and a fast black car split the night northward. Lights burned late in the offices of Eurochem International and worried men sweated in closed offices as the conglomerate moved to crush the occupants of a small yard which stood in the way of future profit.

Tyres revolved silently as the black car, its lights turned off, rolled along Pudding Founders Lane, it eased to a stop opposite number 7, and two dark shadows slid out of it and merged into the gloom of the dark street. They sidled round the corner, and one set about oiling the hinges of the Judas door in one of the large wooden yard gates, while the other inserted two steel probes into the lock. In short order the tumblers clicked into place and the lock turned. They entered stealthily; one drawing a leather bound cosh and brass knuckles from his pocket and the other a small, dull black automatic pistol. They began to tiptoe across the yard from one deep shadow to the next, but stopped suddenly on hearing a noise which sounded like someone rolling barrels across an uneven floor. At the base of the back door was a paler shadow than the rest and the noise came from this. They took another step and the sound increased. One more step and the shadow changed to a barking, snarling blur, all muscle and teeth which hurled itself across the yard at them. The man with the cosh screamed but the other snapped off a shot at the dog as it flew through the air towards his companions' throat. The dog hit the man with the force of a pile driver but the bullet had creased its skull and knocked it out. It rolled off the stricken man and lay on its back on the floor as still as a corpse. Before either man could gather their wits a searing blue flame shot from the darkness and the gun suddenly glowed red hot causing the second miscreant to howl and drop it. As his associate gained his feet a furious ball of claws, beak and feathers slammed into his head tearing at his ski mask and eyes. As he thrashed ineffectually at his winged assailant a ball of yellow fire enveloped the gunman, melting his nylon head gear and setting his trousers alight. This was too much for the pair. Howling and flailing they fled from the yard pursued by winged vengeance and soon the squeal of tyres announced their permanent departure.

Blaggard glided back into the yard to find Sprocket rushing to and fro in panic and whistling plaintively. Mrs Mumbly laid stock still on her side, a pool of blood forming round her head.

"Stop it!" thought the bird sharply. "All this carry on won't help. Is she breathing? Get out the way and let me listen." He cocked his head next to the dog's nose then nodded.

"She's still breathing, but we need to stop the bleeding." He looked at the trembling dragon, "it needs cauterising, a short sharp flame across the wound. Do you understand?" Sprocket stopped shaking and nodded vigorously. He bustled forward, sighted down his beak and shot a lightning fast bolt of white fire at the dogs head. There was a puff of smoke, a sizzle and the dog yelped and jumped up. At the same moment the kitchen door burst open to reveal Brassroyd in nightshirt, cap and boots clutching an antique blunderbuss, the hammer already cocked. He took one look, lowered the hammer placed the gun on the floor and rushed to Mrs Mumbly sweeping her into his arms and hugging her.

"Oh my Lord! What have they done to you?" The dazed dog licked him then lay still as he gently examined the wound on her head.

"This needs a vet. Come on everyone in the kitchen while I phone her." He ushered Sprocket and Blaggard into the warm room shutting the door which made the crow very nervous. Brassroyd placed the dog carefully in her basket and tucked a rug round her, then bustled into the hall and started to dial the vet's number.

"Er, I don't like this" said Blaggard nudging the small dragon. Sprocket understood immediately and nosed open the dog flap so the crow could regain his freedom. "Let me know what happens. I'll be on the pole," and with that he flapped up to his roost.

It had taken Brassroyd only fifteen minutes to put the dog in his van, lock the house and yard and drive to the vets, but she had beaten him to it and had the surgery prepared. With Mrs Mumbly on the table and suitably sedated the vet examined the wound on the dog's head. She x-rayed the skull and declared no fracture. "Heads like bricks this breed," she murmured as she cleaned round the wound. "Neat job of cauterising, did you do it? Saved a lot of bleeding, she'll have a scar but it will probably add to her reputation. After all she's no beauty queen." Mrs Mumbly grumbled in her throat, she was coming out of the anaesthetic and had heard that last remark. "Damn cheek! You're no oil painting yourself," thought the dog.

Sprocket was beside himself with worry by the time Brassroyd and the dog returned. Despite his best efforts, Mrs Mumbly had insisted on walking from the van to the kitchen which gave great relief to the small dragon and the crow on his perch who had watched her stump unsteadily across the yard. The little dragon bounced round the dog whistling excitedly and trying to lick her. Mrs Mumbly put up with this for a time then nosed him over to the basket and tumbled him in. Sprocket lay on his back as the dog gave him a thorough lick wash then rolled over and curled up while she pushed the blanket over him. This done she lay down in front of the range and went to sleep. Satisfied that all was now well, Brassroyd checked the locks and climbed back up stairs to his own bed.

It was gone eight o'clock before anyone stirred the following morning and Blaggard was beginning to worry. This was an early rising house and here it was nearly midday and no-one about. Then the dog flap banged and Sprocket burst into the yard twittering with news. There was a yelp from the inside of the flap and the dragon rushed back to lift the flap and allow Mrs Mumbly to exit without having to use her head to lift it.

"How's the Head?" enquired Blaggard.

"Sore! But nothing a bit of fried bread and some crisp bacon rind won't cure when he drags himself out of bed," Mrs Mumbly retorted.

Sprocket bounced round the yard hoovering up mixed scrap and washing it down with gulps of oily water. He was so pleased that Mrs Mumbly was all right. Every now and then he would rush up to her and rub along her side gurgling softly and the dog would pat him away gently with her paw. The crow flapped down on to the back of an old car seat.

"Have a good scar there when it heals. Make you look a real hard case," he quipped.

"Don't you start; I had enough of that from that young slip of a vet last night. No beauty queen indeed and her with a mouth full of teeth that would do a horse proud." snorted the dog.

"Definitely OK! Back to your normal charming self I see," Blaggard mused.

"May as well be, fat chance of sympathy from a bag of feathers like you."

The friendly insults flew back and forth, a mark of the deep affection they had for each other and the relief that the violence of the previous night had left no lasting damage.

A clattering from the kitchen, followed after some moments by the smell of frying bacon, dragged Mrs Mumbly like iron filings to a magnet and she bade the crow fare well and barked at Sprocket to open the flap for her.

As it was Sunday, Brassroyd fetched the pile of letters from behind the clock and sat down to read his post. First he divided them into three piles, bills, personal and junk. The junk was dealt with easily it went into the secondary burner of the range and quickly added to the general warmth of the kitchen. Personal took a little longer as he read a letter from his sister in Australia, his pen friend in Mallorca and this month's copy of 'Friends of Steam' magazine. Finally he turned to the official pile.

Brassroyd perused the electricity bill. Another month and his combined wind and bio fuel generator would be in operation and he would be selling them electricity. It would be pleasant to receive a cheque rather than a bill. The next two were begging letters from a cat's home and the local cobble stone renovation society. He would send a small donation to the cats if only to keep the dratted felines out of his yard and cobblestones could look after themselves. The large buff envelope with the council crest lay ominously at the bottom of the pile and he picked it up as if it might explode.

What emerged from the envelope should have had a fuse attached, for what it proposed devastated the calm of the kitchen as effectively as a hand grenade. Jumping to his feet Brassroyd uttered a stream of language fit to blister paint, casting doubt on the parentage of various council officials, their spouses and offspring. The letter was headed Environmental Health and Public Safety Department followed by the words Notice of Compulsory Cessation of Trading and Closure. There followed numerous paragraphs of closely typed jargon, which boiled down to a threat to seize his land and property and bulldoze all buildings and structures there on. In small type on the reverse it informed him he had seven days, commencing the previous Wednesday, to lodge an appeal with the Chief Officers Clerk, or demolition would commence forthwith.

CHAPTER 6

The Fight Back Begins

Brassroyd was incandescent with rage. He stormed up and down the kitchen ranting about police states and beaurocratic corruption. When he finally wound down and stopped trying to blister paintwork with profanity he realised he needed help. His nephew Neil worked for the council in some sort of public help department, so he laced his boots, tied his muffler and burst into Sunday morning like a panzer division at the Battle of the Bulge.

Neil lived with several of his mates in a tall, narrow, terraced house in what had once been the posh end of town, but was now a mass of cheap bed sits and low end buy-to-let properties. Despite it being past eleven o'clock by the time Brassroyd reached Neil's front door there was no sign of life. He pounded on the cracked paintwork of the door till several flakes, five spiders and the corroded nought of the number ten fell onto the step. There was a grinding and splintering noise of ancient dirt and paint being disturbed and a bleary eyed face peered out of the upstairs bay window, and a voice thick with sleep asked what the hell the matter was.

Brassroyd looked up to see his bare chested nephew squinting down at him.

"Come on our Neil," boomed Brassroyd. "Get thar bum out o' bed, I need thy help!"

"But its Sunday." moaned the head

"Well tha can't lie stinking in thy pit all weekend. Get down here and let me in, it's perishing on this door step," bellowed Brassroyd.

"OK, keep the noise down. I'll be down in a sec," with that the window closed, and shortly after the door opened to reveal Neil in a pair of boxer shorts.

Brassroyd bustled in and Neil rapidly shut out the cold.

"What's so urgent it won't wait until Monday?" queried Neil.

"This!" said Brassroyd flourishing the Council letter.

Neil glanced at it briefly, shivered and handed it back. "You put the kettle on, I'll put some clothes on then I'll look at it properly." With that he disappeared back up stairs.

When he returned his uncle had made two mugs of steaming tea, washed up the pile in the sink and had the makings of bacon sandwiches sizzling on the stove. Neil picked up the letter and read it through twice.

"Where are the copy of the inspectors report and the notice of intended action?" Neil questioned.

"The what?" asked Brassroyd.

"You should have had a copy of the complaint along with suggested remedial actions before initial inspection was carried out," said Neil. "That's followed by the initial report and a six week remediation period so you can clean up any remaining mess. A final inspection then takes place and only then if the environmental threat still exists is an application made to the magistrate's court for a Clearance and Rectification Order. You must have been given a hearing date to attend court?"

"NO!" said Brassroyd.

"But they have to do all that before a letter like this can be issued and you should get a copy of the final report and the court order so you can appeal. Its standard procedure, laid down in the Local Government Environmental Safety Act of 2001, Neil explained.

"I aint ad none o' that." stated Brassroyd.

"Then it's illegal." said Neil.

"Good, so I needn't worry, I can chuck it on fire." smiled his uncle.

"Hang on," said Neil "being illegal will mean very little if they bulldoze the yard and number seven on Wednesday. You'd have to prove that none of the procedures had happened; you didn't receive the necessary paperwork and if they have copies on file how would you do that? Can you afford a lawyer because you can bet they can and will have the very best legal representation?"

His nephew paced back and forth taking ferocious bites from a bacon sandwich as delicate as a doorstep.

"This stinks!" exclaimed Neil.

"Well the bacon smelled all right when I got it out the fridge." muttered Brassroyd.

"Not the butty." muttered Neil, his mouth full of bread and bacon. "This letter, at short notice, and no preamble. You sure there's been nothing else regarding the yard?"

"Only a silly offer to buy me out from the stink works next door. They're the environmental hazard if anyone is," replied his uncle.

"I can't get at the council records till I'm in work tomorrow and what we want won't be available on the public website. We need a back door into this and someone with very special IT skills, and I know just the man, Nerdy Dave. Spends so much time in front of a VDU his specs have gone square. Hang on, I'll get my mobile and ring him," Neil returned with an old Nokia.

"I thought you had one of them all singing all dancing modern ones?" said his uncle "3T or something?"

"I do, but Dave's modifying it and it's 3G. He's lent me this old one to tide me over; this is his own invention 3P."

"What's that then?" asked Brassroyd.

"P stands for piggy back. It hunts for an ongoing call then piggy backs onto it so you don't get charged. Means your call stops when the carrier stops but starts again when it finds another. You can talk all day, and it costs you nothing. The software even remembers numbers which make

long calls and scans them first. Nerdy Dave's got all sorts of brill phone and computer mods and can go through computer security faster than a bad kebab on a Saturday night," laughed Neil

Neil dialled a number, waited, then spoke in what appeared to be text speak for thirty seconds then switched off.

"He said to come round in half an hour when he's up and dressed."

They finished breakfast then went out to Neil's old but immaculate Ford Escort for the drive over to Lower Scrotley where Nerdy Dave lived in a derelict sheep fold, which he maintained he was doing up though it looked more ramshackle every time Neil saw it.

"When we've seen your mate I've summat at t' yard I want thee to see," muttered Brassroyd.

"OK." Said Neil "I'll drop you back at the yard when we're done."

He concentrated on the narrow roads across the moor top and down to Scrotley Dale. The view should have been magnificent but, due to the low cloud and incessant drizzle, all that could be seen was rough grass, bogs, rocks and wind blasted thorn trees.

Lower Scrotley differed from Upper Scrotley in that people still lived there. Decades ago the inhabitants of Top End as the locals called it had given up the one sided struggle against wind, rain and terminal foot rot and moved further down the valley or somewhere less depressing entirely.

Nerdy Dave's place was down a rutted track a hundred yards past the last cottage, and Neil drove carefully down the potholed lane stopping the car on an area of gravel outside the front door.

Brassroyd was amazed that anyone lived in the hovel which seemed to grow from a junk pile that made his yard seem the epitome of organisation. Neil opened the low door and they ducked into a cross between a star ship flight deck and The Old Curiosity Shop. There was a smell of last nights' dinner and old socks. In front of a bank of monitors was a pile of old blankets. Old and decrepit as the shack was the technology was state of the art. The blankets stirred and a tousled head peered at them through wire rimmed glasses.

"What's your problem?" asked Dave and Neil handed him Brassroyd's letter.

"Ah! Need some back door background. Come to the right place you have." Without further ado Dave began clattering at his keyboard and mouse while the main screen showed, first the council logo then a series of security screens, which he went through like a hot knife through butter. In short order he went from main listings, to Environmental Health and Safety, to Enforcement and finally Action files. Dave located the file concerning Brassroyd's yard, opened it and whistled.

"You're down for demolition and no appeal. Serious biohazard. Immediate action, total containment and decontamination. What you got down there, an unshielded nuclear waste dump?" queried Dave.

"No, just a scrap yard." said Neil. "Can you backtrack this without leaving footprints and find who is at the bottom of it?"

"No probs. Take a bit of time is all. Make a cuppa while I get stuck in." With that Dave got down to some serious hacking. As he worked, a printer to one side whirred and spat out page after page of official looking documents. Occasionally Dave would pause and read something on one of the screens and mutter things like "Nasty" or "Seriously bad" or "Evil devils"

Neil made the tea and set a mug by Dave's elbow, and then he and Brassroyd sat sipping theirs while Dave worked on.

Brassroyd nudged Neil "How's he power all this? Must cost him a fortune in electric, and I never seen no power lines to this place."

"All his own power." said Neil. "Solar panels, wind turbines, a small hydro unit in the stream at the back and a bio digester which eats all his waste and produces methane for a converted diesel generator. All backed up by a stack of old car batteries in the pig shed for storage. It all goes through a huge rotary converter which gives him AC for this lot.

"But how did he get this place?" Brassroyd asked.

"Bought it at auction for next to nothing when the old bloke, who owned it and half the moor, popped his clogs and no one else was interested. Had it about three years now, makes a living debugging computer games and other software. He could make a fortune but he says he's not into capitalism. So he lives out here, communes with nature and recycles anything and everything. Most of this stuff is ex military, American or Jap specials, but he links it up in interesting ways the manufacturers never dreamed of and runs his own software. Bit of a genius really but nobody would employ him he's too weird and will only work on what interests him at the moment."

At that point Dave yawned, stretched and picking up a pile of paper from the printer turned to face the waiting pair.

"This is seriously corrupt stuff." he said dumping the documents in front of Neil and Brassroyd. "Your place is next to Eurochem right?"

"Right" they answered in unison.

"It's them what wants your yard. Right in the corner you got a ventilation shaft to the old Bradley Festering deep mine, must go down a thousand feet at least into workings abandoned in the 1920s and that's what they're after."

"But how'd yer find that out?" Brassroyd wanted to know.

"Once I found Eurochem it was easy. That lot have been riding rough shod over planning and industrial safety regulations for the last fifty years, worst accident record in this country possibly the world. Biggest bunch of crooks in business today. Too clever for their own good and as tight fisted as hell. As a consequence they run their IT security on the cheap, it's so full of holes a school kid could drive a coach and horses through it. What you have there is a complete record of board decisions to dump toxic waste down your mine vent. Listings of council officials bribed or blackmailed and a timetable for how long it will take to turn that eyesore next to your yard from an economic basket case to a thumping big profit. All that stands in their way is Brassroyd Environmental and the bulldozers roll at 8am Monday morning," explained Dave.

"But the letter says I have till Wednesday." wailed Brassroyd. "What on earth can I do between now and then?"

"Quite a lot." said Dave grinning like a Cheshire Cat. "Neil, you know the councillors and there's a list of their email addresses. I've set up a press release you can send to all the ones who are likely to do something useful. Use that laptop, the send email address and service provider is untraceable and will destruct as soon as you're finished. I've sent a similar one to all the main papers, TV and Radio stations and also the stock exchange. That should keep the board of Eurochem up to their necks in muck and bullets for at least a week denying all the rumours and allegations.

Meantime we go back to the yard and set in for a siege.

While Neil sent the emails Dave filled a large rucksack with technology then closed down all his systems. Groping behind a pile of wires and plugs he fished out a padabag and threw it to Neil. "Here you go, all set up for 3P so no more phone bills. You can also take movies up to fifteen minutes long on the camera and it's got a decent zoom lens too."

"Thanks mate," said Neil stuffing the phone in his pocket and heading for the car followed by Brassroyd, while Dave locked up and set his security system.

The weather was no better on the return journey and it was getting dark by the time they reached the outskirts of Batherby Bridge. The fog flowing down from the fells hid the huge multi wheeled transporters with their loads of giant bulldozers and earth movers which were creeping up on the unsuspecting town. Neil stopped the car and Brassroyd got out to open the gates. Neil parked the car and he and Dave waited by the back door as the old man closed and locked the gates. As soon as the back door was opened an ecstatic Mrs Mumbly cannoned into Neil, her greeting causing him to double up clutching his delicate parts as the dog did her best to lick him all over.

"I love you dearly but I do wish you wouldn't do that every time I come round" groaned Neil, wiping the tears of pain from his eyes. Mrs Mumbly rolled onto her back to have her belly tickled and her tail beat a tattoo on the stone floor.

While Neil was recovering, in the London headquarters of Eurochem things were going from bad to worse. Half an hour before the phones had started ringing and now the switchboard was jammed with journalists demanding reactions and answers to information leaked and questions raised in a damning email which had lit up news desk screens across the world. Already the Eurochem share price had halved in opening trading on the Tokyo stock exchange. The managing director was incandescent with rage and the senior partners of Grasping, Myther and Pire had been summoned and ordered to issue writs against everyone and anyone who had sent the email. The problem was that no one had, at least it could not be traced back to anyone. Whatever the IT department tried, the trail simply faded into cyber space. The only thing for sure was that the sending address could only be tracked back to the United States, 'State Department's' main computer, and you could hardly sue them. Archibald Grasping pointed this fact out to the board and received a collection of withering stares in response. "You will have to call off the demolition. If the press get hold of that on top of what they are already chasing you will be finished in The City."

The chairman glared at the lawyer. "We can't. Without that site and its vent shaft this company will drown in its own toxic waste. Storage is impossibly expensive and we have no capital reserves left to fund it. We have been running on false promises for so long that if we don't move now the entire international operation will collapse like a house of cards. So we go ahead. You have all the records of our dealings with the council? Well use them to put some iron in their back bones and our PR consultants can earn their inflated fees for the next forty eight hours after which we will have our licence to print money and no one will give a damn what happens to that benighted back water. So get out of here and do what you're paid for," he snarled.

The meeting broke up and worried men and women hurried off to fire fight and stall the worlds press.

The fact that no one was taking any notice of his pain brought Neil back to reality, and he looked up from his hunched position to see what was more important. He followed Dave's riveted gaze, and was immediately focused on the small trembling creature that had just appeared round the corner of the large black range.

"What on earth is that?" whispered Dave. Neil just stared in blank amazement.

"Ah, that's what I wanted you t' see when we got back here. It's a scrap dragon," Brassroyd declared.

"A what?" both boys gasped.

"A scrap dragon, Dracus, Metalicus, Trogladytees, to give him his proper title, but whether it's a greater or lesser remains to be seen. Can't tell till they're older," quoted Brassroyd from his previous studies.

Both lads looked from the dragon to Brassroyd then back to the dragon.

"But they're not real, just a myth, dragons don't exist," yammered Neil.

"Well that one does and his name is Sprocket," Brassroyd bent down and held out a handful of rusty washers. The little creature waddled forward emitting small puffs of pink steam from its beak and hoovered up the proffered titbit. Mrs Mumbly rolled over and began to lick the little dragon who, vibrating with pleasure, emitted pink smoke rings and small yipps.

"That's amazing. Can it breathe fire?" both lads wanted to know.

"Most definitely. Hot enough to cut steel. He's also fast enough to catch that stinking cat from next door and trim its mangy fur," said Brassroyd, with an expression of pride on his face.

CHAPTER 7

Battle Lines are Drawn

As the dusk gathered outside, a convoy of large articulated lorries swept off the motorway and proceeded to wind its way up the narrow road towards Batherby Bridge. They moved like a giant, segmented snake and it was obvious to anyone who saw them pass that they were not on an errand of peace and mercy. There was an expanse of waste ground on the edge of the town where the old shunting yard used to be and the trucks pulled onto this and started to unload their cargos of bulldozers, and cranes with pneumatic drills and ripping claws. One or two local lads came to marvel at the size of the machines but were hurried off by men with large, savage dogs, closer to wolves than any domestic breed. They ran off to tell their friends what was happening and soon a collection of children were hurling questions and abuse at the menacing guards.

Neil was standing on the front step of number seven staring at the low glowering clouds, trying to get his head round dragons suddenly coming into his life, when a gaggle of small boys came round the corner from the tow path laughing and joking about how brave they had been with the guard dogs.

"Hey mister, you should see the huge machines coming off lorries down at the sidings!" shouted one of the lads.

Neil, jerked from his doorstep reverie, called the group over and questioned them about what was happening at the abandoned shunting yard. On learning the details he rushed back to the kitchen to inform Dave and Brassroyd what was going on. After a hurried conversation they put Mrs Mumbly on her lead, gathered up Sprocket in a blanket, and after locking the front door half walked, half ran to the sidings to see for themselves. By the time they got there it was past eleven o'clock and the children had dispersed and a steel tube and wire mesh security fence had been erected round the yard. Inside could clearly be seen six large bull dozers and an assortment of self propelled cranes with demolition devices attached to the end of their jibs.

"Going a bit over the top for one small cottage and a half an acre of scrap yard aint they?" muttered Brassroyd.

"Well they certainly mean business. I'll go and ask that security guard by the gate what's going on," said Neil and wandered over to the gate as if he hadn't a care in the world.

After a muttered conversation with the night watchman he returned with the news that there would be no action till the morning when the big boss from London turned up to supervise. They decided to go back to number 7 and see what they could do to organise a demonstration for the following morning. When they arrived back they let the dog off her lead, put the dragon in his basket and retired to the front parlour to make calls and send emails to anyone they could think of who might help.

Mrs Mumbly was in no mood for sleeping, and nudging Sprocket out of his basket, went out through the flap in the back door closely followed by the dragon. Blaggard was bouncing up and down on his telephone pole.

"Have you seen em? Have you seen what's going on down at the sidings? What are we going to do?" were his furious thoughts.

They gathered together by the fence and Mrs. Mumbly explained her plan of action. This done Blaggard flew off to gather as many crows as possible, while dog and dragon squeezed through the gap in the fence and set off for the shunting yard.

On arrival Mrs Mumbly rapidly dug a hole under the security fence and the pair scrambled through. As they set off for the giant machines the little dragon turned and flamed the hole so that they left no scent, he also puffed hot steam on their path for the same reason as they made their way across the compound. At the first machine the dog showed the dragon the connecting bolts of the caterpillar tracks and he burnt them through with jets of pale blue fire. They then scrabbled up onto the machine and after Sprocket dissolved the lock on the cab by carefully dribbling on it he went inside and welded all the control pedals and levers together. Out of the sky swooped a large flock of crows and a few inquisitive owls that were up for any nocturnal fun going. Each carried a tree seed in its beak and one of the dragon pellets from the bag and the bin at the scrap yard. On landing by several of the trucks they scuttled underneath and dug a small hole with beak and claw. Into the holes they dropped a dragon pellet and a seed, an acorn here, a sycamore there. Here a pine cone, there a conker, these they then carefully covered over. Unseen by the security guard, dog, dragon and birds scurried around the yard for over an hour then silently left.

The following morning woke to a determined drizzle which soaked paperboys and did its best to turn the first postal delivery of the day into papier-mâché. After a hurried breakfast and very little sleep the group exiting number 7 Pudding Founders Lane were not in the best of tempers. They trudged along under dripping brollies, the dog with her tail between her legs and dragon with only its nose poking out of the neck of Brassroyd's rain cape. On arrival at the shunting yard they were greeted by a sight to stop the world and utter pandemonium. The yard which before the trucks had parked there had been barren land with a few scrubby thorn bushes and rank grass was now a forest of vigorous and mature trees, cranes and bulldozers lay on their sides or upside down their tracks hanging off. Through any gap or window thick branches curled and the articulated lorries were torn and twisted out of all recognition by the verdant growth. Men ran around, dogs barked, and in the middle a large purple faced man was screaming at anyone and everyone while kicking his large black limousine in a fit of uncontrolled temper. All this was proving very entertaining to the large crowd which had gathered in answer to Neil and Dave's emails and phone calls. They waved their placards and chanted and sang, and were generally having a whale of a time at the expense of the luckless men in the compound. News crews turned up, and the purple faced man turned his rage on them and proceeded to show the entire country the bullying foulmouthed face at the top of Eurochem International. Eventually he was bundled back into the black limousine by his minions, kicking, punching and swearing, till the heavy door closed cutting off the tirade and the car drove away to a chorus of boos and cat calls from the crowd.

The drizzle finally drove the crowds away, and the news net works, having exhausted the increasingly bizarre explanations for the overnight appearance of a forest, packed up and went back to their studios to feed on the much richer news of the chaos that the impending collapse of a multinational chemical giant was having on the stock market. After dropping the dog and dragon back at the yard, Brassroyd took Neil and Dave for a celebratory drink at the Furnace Raddlers Arms.

CHAPTER 8

An End to Hostilities

As far as Mrs Mumbly was concerned the battle and the day were far from over. She and Sprocket went out into the yard and while the dragon hunted for snacks among the piles of scrap, dog and crow planned the next stage of the campaign. The crow flew off to gather his squadrons for the nights work and while birds swooped and soared, scratched and scrabbled at every patch of bare earth throughout the Eurochem complex the dragon gorged himself on scrap. Piles of pellets grew in the yard and were carried away by crows, owls and an increasing number of other bird species to be buried along with seeds all around the chemical works. Before Brassroyd returned from the celebration, dog and dragon were curled up in their basket warmly steaming off a damp evening's work in front of the range. The birds had dispersed and Blaggard had returned for a well deserved sleep on his telephone pole. As the night wore on and the rain fell on Batherby Bridge the only sounds to be heard were the crack of brick, the groan of branch and the rumble of falling masonry.

The night shift at the chemical works had been laid off some weeks before, due to the build up of toxic waste, and when the day shift arrived, in the grey light of morning, they stood at what remained of the factory gates and stared at the mass of trees, fallen brickwork and twisted girders which was all that remained of the Eurochem site. When the news broke Eurochem's shares went into free fall and by lunch time the company had been declared bankrupt. Very few workers were out of a job as most of the factories were so automated, but a stream of bemused executives could be seen leaving the London offices carrying cardboard boxes full of their belongings.

The press had a field day as more of Eurochem's working practices became common knowledge. Writs were issued for contamination of various parts of the country where toxic waste had been dumped. High Court injunctions were sought to try and hide what had been going on and a number of very embarrassed local authority councillors and officials faced a barrage of awkward questions about their dealings with the collapsed company. Resignations were tendered and rapidly accepted, but journalists could smell blood and it became obvious that simply resigning was not going to fend off retribution through the courts.

CHAPTER 9

Meet the Relations

While the City of London fought like vultures over a corpse, in Batherby Bridge the town was alive with workers clearing the mess left by the sites collapse.

Brassroyd sat in the kitchen wondering what to do next when the dog and dragon bounded in from the yard and began to myther and worry him to get up and come with them outside. When it became clear that if he didn't move he was likely to lose his trouser leg, he grabbed his cap and jacket and followed them into the yard. Mrs Mumbly and Sprocket nudged and harried him towards the van and when he opened the door, they jumped onto the passenger seat and looked at him expectantly. He started the van then went and opened the gate into the lane. Returning to the van he manoeuvred it out of the gate, then closed and securely locked it behind them. They set off with the dog giving directions by pointing her head and barking as they approached a turn or junction.

In this manner they left town and wound their way towards the top of the fells.

As evening fell they bumped and bounced along a rutted track towards a marker showing the highest point on the moor. On reaching it Brassroyd pulled the van to a halt and the three got out. Sprocket flapped and scrabbled onto the top of the van then sat up on its hind legs. Stretching his neck and pointing his nose to the sky he emitted a high pitched bubbling whistle. Nothing happened. Again he stretched and this time whistled louder and longer. Looking round from the vantage point Brassroyd could just make out black dots converging through the darkening sky. These became crows and owls which swooped down and settled in a large circle around the van and stared at the sky. The little dragon stretched higher almost on tip toe with its stubby wings spread out and again emitted its strange warbling call. This time it went on for nearly five minutes. In the eerie silence that followed the world seemed to hold its breath and every creature searched the gloomy sky. Suddenly their eyes were drawn to a swirling in the clouds. It dropped lower and lower till it touched the ground and stayed there gradually thinning. Sprocket became very excited bouncing up and down on the van roof and giving short squeaks and puffs of pink steam. Finally the mist began to clear and revealed a group of twenty large dragons which seemed to shimmer with all the colours of the rainbow. One of the largest dragons left the group and stalked towards the van, stopping some yards from it.

Sprocket stretched his neck towards the enormous creature and it bent its own neck and nuzzled the little one.

Brassroyd stood open mouthed as a deep voice resonated in his mind.

"Thank you for bringing our little brother to meet us," was echoed in Brassroyd's mind. "It's a pleasure I'm sure," stammered the man.

"We heard his call clearly here, away from the overwhelming noise of human thought," was what Brassroyd heard.

Mrs Mumbly wagged her tail and the large dragon bent lower and rubbed his muzzle against hers and she gave it a friendly lick. The other dragons came forward, one at a time and nuzzled the baby scrap dragon and the dog, while filling Brassroyd's mind with their names and making soft chuckling sounds in their throats.

When all had introduced themselves the big dragon spoke again in the man's mind.

"All can hear my words as you can in their own language and all can understand me. The small one you call Sprocket has explained your problems and we can offer a solution. The old mine workings below your yard and the surrounding area will be a perfect working place for a number of his kind. During the day they will help to process your waste materials into useful items and raw materials for use in other industries. At night they will leave the workings to fly free above the Great Northern forest which your friends the birds will plant using the spoil pellets from the scrap dragons to give it a head start. It will take many years to complete this task as the dragons must work out of sight, and conveyer systems will need to be built to take waste in and product out, but together we will overcome these obstacles. Now take our little friend and your trusty dog back to your home while the birds and my dragons make a start on the forest"

Brassroyd bowed to the large dragon and muttered his thanks. He scooped up Sprocket who, so tired by all the excitement, went fast asleep in his arms. Mrs Mumbly climbed into the van and Brassroyd placed the little dragon on the passenger seat where she curled up around it. He started the van and waving out of the window to the birds and dragons drove slowly back to Batherby Bridge.

CHAPTER 10
The Great Northern Forest

In the following months no one noticed the skyline of the fell become fuzzy with new growth, and those hardy souls who did venture onto the high moor passed by the new sprouting trees with hardly a glance. As the weeks flew by, people noticed the small woods in the valleys and dips on the moor but presumed they had always been there and simply hadn't seen them before. Families started to go up for picnics and enjoy the shade on hot days in the summer and as the trees spread and the woods joined up, the high moor, which for so long had been a barren wilderness, became a playground for the local villages. Any litter left lying around vanished during the night and anyone trying to use the woods for criminal purposes received a visit from a vision so terrible they left the area suddenly and never returned. Lost children always found their way back to their parents with tales of following small dragons or crows which hopped along the ground, but they were never believed. After all everyone knew that dragons were things of myths and fairy tales and crows were solitary creatures who keep well away from people. So the trees grew and increased in number.

At Brassroyd Environmental things were very busy. The company was growing with both Neil and Dave joining the work force and the new products for refreshing tired gardens proved increasingly popular. Neil worked with the dragons improving the mine workings and building the tunnels to the old station, which was expanding with the growing number of trains bringing scrap and waste in and taking garden products out. Dave set up an online business to sell their catalogue of garden ware, and week by week added new items as the burgeoning units on the once declining industrial estate found new uses for the raw materials the dragons produced. There were speculative rumours about where the raw materials came from and where all the scrap went, but most people were just glad to have interesting and well paid jobs and the few who talked of seeing huge winged lizards in the sky on clear nights were dismissed as being too fond of beer or indulging in nefarious substances. An increasing number of people were coming into contact with the dragons but after the first shock of meeting a large winged lizard that spoke in their minds they found them fascinating and kept the secret of the dragons safe. Ever since men had gone into the dark places underground there had been legends of fantastic creatures of the dark and the deep. Well, who would believe them anyway?

It would be nice to say that they all lived happily ever after but the world is not like that. There are too many dark places where evil can sink its stinking roots into society and poison people's lives. There are too many greedy individuals who will go to any lengths and grind their fellow humans under foot to gather greater and greater wealth. Look out for more adventures with the team from number 7 Pudding Founders Lane as they go out into the world to right wrongs.

LIST OF
CHARACTERS AND PLACES

Arthur Kitchener Mountbatten Brassroyd: Owner of Brassroyd Environmental.

Neil Robert Brassroyd: Son of Frederick Lebassy Windsor Brassroyd and Eleanor (Nelly) Threepstock both deceased, and nephew of Arthur.

Postlethwait Runswick Mountstaff: landlord of the Furnace Raddlers Arms (est. 1839).

Bethesda Euphemia Mountstaff: Wife of Mountstaff and maker of the best pie and peas in the north and a horse radish sauce so hot you could weld with it.

Aristotle Portnoy (Pongo) Feather: Owner of Feather's Pharmacy (est. 1906) Steam and Brass Band enthusiast and Brassroyd's best friend since school days.

Cheryl Tracy Clout: Counter assistant in the Pharmacy and gossip

David Bertwhistle: (Nerdy Dave) IT genius and Neil's friend. He is a master of mobile communications and the internet.

Mrs. Mumbly: An English bull terrier belonging to Brassroyd (though she believes that Brassroyd belongs to her). She found the dragon egg and has brought Sprocket up like her own pup. Now she has five proper pups of her own.

Blaggard: A crow who perches on the telephone pole on the towpath of the canal by the fence of the scrap yard. He thinks he is occult and connected to the dark arts. Really he's just a large black bird with an over active imagination.

Sprocket: A lesser scrap dragon hatched from an egg in the Kitchen at 7 Pudding Founders Lane.

Golden Friend: A large golden coloured dragon who comes in answer to Sprocket's call.

Batherby Bridge: Once the centre of the Five Fells region and a flourishing market town. Now it is a run down, post industrial back water with few prospects and fewer jobs.

7 Pudding Founders Lane: The only house on Pudding Founders Lane. With its attached scrap yard it is sandwiched between number 3 and 4 plants of Eurochem. Nobody can

remember if there were ever other houses on the lane. Or what pudding founders were or did.

Furnace Raddlers Arms: a local ale house owned by Mountstaff the landlord. Has a few regular drinkers including Brassroyd and offers the best Pie and Peas in the North.

Eurochem: A huge multinational chemical company teetering on the brink of collapse due to the cost of storage and disposal of vast quantities of toxic waste. It needs Brassroyd's yard for the mine air shaft in one corner down which it could dump its chemical waste.

The Great Northern Forest: nonexistent at the start of the story, it comes about thanks to the crows, other birds and the fertilising properties of Scrap dragon pellets.

DRAGON FACTS

1. Do Dragons eat people or animals? No, they are vegetarians. In general with the exception of the various types of Scrap Dragons who eat industrial waste and lick minerals from rocks.

2. Are Dragons bad and cruel? No, they are normally shy and non-violent unless their young ones or eggs are attacked, in which the females can become very aggressive, but this is the same for all creatures.

3. Dragons have on average 14 stomachs to separate solids, liquids and generate gases for lift and fire. They also have at least 5 or more gas bladders which give them lift and provide the fuel for their fire.

4. Dragon's bones are made of laminated calcium and carbon foamed with helium. This makes them both light and strong. Laminated means made of thin strips held together with glue, in the case of dragons this is thin strips of sinew.

5. There are no dragon fossils because when a dragon dies (and they live for hundreds of years) the helium in their bones and scales evaporates and all that is left is dust which blows away in the wind.

6. Where do dragons come from? Not even dragons know. It is like the question, what came first? The chicken or the egg?

7. Dragons are trans dimensional creatures and can pass between worlds.

8. Do all dragons fly? Yes, some better than others. The larger ones use their huge wings and fly like birds. The smaller ones, like Scrap Dragons who have small stubby wings use jet propulsion from flight ducts just above the base of their tails.

9. Can Scrap Dragons eat anything? Yes with the exception of liquorice which gives them violent hiccups and has led to towns being burned down in the past.

10. Have dragons ever been common? Yes, back in the time of the dinosaurs there were lots of them and pterodactyls were a cross breed. But though they out-lived the giant reptiles they retreated to another dimension because of persecution by man.

CONTACT DETAILS

email: penworkspublishing@gmail.com
http://bryanpentelow.wix.com/bryan-pentelow

If you have any questions, find me on facebook and post them on my page or send me an email. I will do my best to answer them and if I don't know the answers I will ask Mr. Brassroyd if I can have a look at some of his many old and dusty books about Dragons and if that fails I will ask Sprocket.

If your questions are about dogs or crows I will ask Sprocket as he can talk to Mrs. Mumbly and Blaggard, unfortunately I can't.

Best Regards
Bryan Pentelow (Dragon Friend)

Printed in Great Britain
by Amazon

22618913R00065